Groundwood Books / House of Anansi Press
110 Spadina Avenue, Suite 801, Toronto, Ontario M5V 2K4
Distributed in the USA by Publishers Group West
1700 Fourth Street, Berkeley, CA 94710

We acknowledge for their financial support of our publishing program
the Canada Council for the Arts, the Government of Canada through
the Book Publishing Industry Development Program (BPIDP) and the
Ontario Arts Council.

ONTARIO ARTS COUNCIL
CONSEIL DES ARTS DE L'ONTARIO

Library and Archives Canada Cataloguing in Publication
Clark, Joan
Snow / by Joan Clark; pictures by Kady MacDonald Denton.
ISBN-13: 978-0-88899-712-8
ISBN-10: 0-88899-712-4
I. Denton, Kady MacDonald II. Title.
PS8555.L37S66 2006   jC813'.54   C2005-907882-0

The illustrations are in watercolor and ink on Arches hot-press watercolor paper with some oil stick and charcoal.

Printed and bound in China

For Sammy

SNOW

Joan Clark PICTURES BY Kady MacDonald Denton

GROUNDWOOD BOOKS
HOUSE OF ANANSI PRESS
TORONTO BERKELEY

ONE MORNING Sammy got out
of bed and saw thick snow falling.

The snow covered the trees and grass.
It blew against windows and doors.

It snowed through breakfast, lunch and supper.

It snowed through play time
and read time.

It snowed through bed time,
sleep time and dream time.

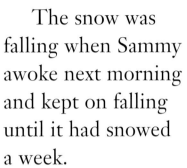

The snow was falling when Sammy awoke next morning and kept on falling until it had snowed a week.

It didn't stop but kept on falling until it had snowed a month.

One morning Sammy looked
through a peephole in the window
and saw that the snow had stopped.
    The world was completely covered
in snow.

Trees and houses disappeared.
Shovelers and plows appeared.
The shovelers made tiny paths through
the snow. The plows pushed the snow into
peaks and cliffs.

Sammy put on his jacket and boots, went outside and climbed the highest mountain, which happened to be the roof of his house.

When he reached the top, he looked down. Around him were other mountains, smoke curling skyward from a few.

Sammy imagined what was beneath the snow.

He imagined a huge black bear
and her cubs inside a snow cave.
Whales and seals swimming in
arctic pools.

He imagined a wooly mammoth
and a ship locked in ice.

He imagined people in parkas building igloos.

Santa in his workshop making toys.

Dwarves and elves mining rubies and emeralds.

Moles drinking ice-cream sodas and iced tea.

Every morning Sammy trudged up the mountain and imagined what was beneath the snow.

Every morning the sun poured down its warmth and melted the snow.

Trickles and streams ran down the mountainside. The mountain became smaller and smaller.

Peaks and cliffs disappeared. Rooftops and trees appeared.

Until one day Sammy stood in the warm
sunshine on an island of snow surrounded by
puddles of water and slush.

His mother opened the window and said,
"What are you doing out there, Sammy?"

Sammy smiled at her dreamily and said, "Imagining grass."